PENGUIN BOOKS

THE GREEN MILE: PART 1
THE TWO DEAD GIRLS

Stephen King, one of the world's bestselling writers, was born in Portland, Maine, in 1947, and was educated at the University of Maine at Orono. He shot to fame with the publication of his first novel, *Carrie*, and his subsequent titles include *The Shining* and *Misery*, which have all been made into highly successful films. He lives with his wife, the novelist Tabitha King, and their three children in Bangor, Maine.

Watch out for Stephen King's *Rose Madder*, out soon in paperback from New English Library, and his new novel *Desperation*, coming shortly in hardback from Hodder & Stoughton.

STEPHEN KING

The Green Mile

PART ONE

The Two Dead Girls

with a Foreword by the Author

PENGUIN BOOKS

PENGUIN BOOKS

Published by the Penguin Group
Penguin Books Ltd, 27 Wrights Lane, London W8 5TZ, England
Penguin Books USA Inc., 375 Hudson Street, New York, New York 10014, USA
Penguin Books Australia Ltd, Ringwood, Victoria, Australia
Penguin Books Canada Ltd, 10 Alcorn Avenue, Toronto, Ontario, Canada M4V 3B2
Penguin Books (NZ) Ltd, 182–190 Wairau Road, Auckland 10, New Zealand

Penguin Books Ltd, Registered Offices: Harmondsworth, Middlesex, England

Published simultaneously in the USA in Signet and
in Great Britain in Penguin Books 1996
3 5 7 9 10 8 6 4

Printed in England by Clays Ltd, St Ives plc

Foreword: A Letter

October 27, 1995

Dear Constant Reader,

Life is a capricious business. The story which begins in this little book exists in this form because of a chance remark made by a realtor I have never met. This happened a year ago, on Long Island. Ralph Vicinanza, a long-time friend and business associate of mine (what he does mostly is to sell foreign publishing rights for books and stories), had just rented a house there. The realtor remarked that the house "looked like something out of a story by Charles Dickens."

The remark was still on Ralph's mind when he welcomed his first houseguest, British publisher Malcolm Edwards. He repeated it to Edwards, and they began chatting about Dickens. Edwards mentioned that Dickens had published many of his novels in installments, either folded into magazines or by themselves as chapbooks (I don't know the origin of this word, meaning a smaller-than-average book, but have always loved its air of intimacy and friendliness). Some of the novels, Edwards added, were actually written and revised in the shadow of publication; Charles Dickens was one novelist apparently not afraid of a deadline.

Dickens's serialized novels were immensely popular; so popular, in fact, that one of them precipitated a tragedy in Baltimore. A large group of Dickens fans crowded onto a waterfront dock, anticipating the arrival of an English ship with copies of the final installment of *The Old Curiosity Shop* on board. According to the story, several would-be readers were jostled into the water and drowned.

I don't think either Malcolm or Ralph wanted anyone drowned, but they were curious as to what would happen if serial publication were tried again today. Neither was immediately aware that it has happened (there really is nothing new under the sun) on at least two occasions. Tom Wolfe published the first draft of his novel *Bonfire of the Vanities* serially in *Rolling Stone* magazine, and Michael McDowell (*The Amulet, Gilded Needles, The Elementals*, and the screenplay *Beetlejuice*) published a novel called *Blackwater* in paperback installments. That novel—a horror story about a Southern family with the unpleasant familial trait of turning into alligators—was not McDowell's best, but enjoyed good success for Avon Books, all the same.

The two men further speculated about what might happen if a writer of popular fiction were to try issuing a novel in chapbook editions today—little paperbacks that might sell for a pound or two in Britain, or perhaps three dollars in America (where most paperbacks now sell for $6.99 or $7.99). Someone like Stephen King might make an interesting go of such an experiment, Malcolm said, and from there the conversation moved on to other topics.

Ralph more or less forgot the idea, but it recurred to him in the fall of 1995, following his return from the Frankfurt Book Fair, a kind of international trade show where every day is a showdown for foreign agents like Ralph. He broached the serialization/ chapbook idea to me along with a number of other matters, most of which were automatic turndowns.

The chapbook idea was not an automatic turndown, though; unlike the interview in the Japanese *Playboy* or the all-expenses-paid tour of the Baltic Republics, it struck a bright spark in my imagination. I don't think that I am a modern Dickens—if such a person exists, it is probably John Irving or Salman Rushdie—but I have always loved stories told in episodes. It is a format I first encountered in *The Saturday Evening Post*, and I liked it because the end of each episode made the reader an almost equal participant with the writer—you had a whole week to try to figure out the next twist of the snake. Also, one read and experienced these stories more *intensely*, it seemed to me, because they were rationed. You couldn't gulp, even if you wanted to (and if the story was good, you did).

Best of all, in my house we often read them

aloud—my brother, David, one night, myself the next, my mother taking a turn on the third, then back to my brother again. It was a rare chance to enjoy a written work as we enjoyed the movies we went to and the TV programs (*Rawhide*, *Bonanza*, *Route 66*) that we watched together; they were a family event. It wasn't until years later that I discovered Dickens's novels had been enjoyed by families of his day in much the same fashion, only their fireside agonizings over the fate of Pip and Oliver and David Copperfield went on for *years* instead of a couple of months (even the longest of the *Post* serials rarely ran much more than eight installments).

There was one other thing that I liked about the idea, an appeal that I suspect only the writer of suspense tales and spooky stories can fully appreciate: in a story which is published in installments, the writer gains an ascendancy over the reader which he or she cannot otherwise enjoy: simply put, Constant Reader, you cannot flip ahead and see how matters turn out.

I still remember walking into our living room once when I was twelve or so and seeing my mother in her favorite rocker, peeking at the end of an Agatha Christie paperback while her finger held her actual place around page 50. I was appalled, and told her so (I was twelve, remember, an age at which boys first dimly begin to realize that they know everything), suggesting that reading the end of a mystery novel before you actually get there was on a par with eating the white stuff out of the middle of Oreo cookies and then throwing the cookies themselves away. She laughed her wonderful unembarrassed laugh and said perhaps that was so, but sometimes she just couldn't resist the temptation. Giving in to temptation was a concept I could understand; I had plenty of my own, even at twelve. But here, at last, is an amusing cure for that temptation. Until the final episode arrives in bookstores, no one is going to know how *The Green Mile* turns out ... and that may include me.

Although there was no way he could have known it, Ralph Vicinanza mentioned the idea of a novel in installments at what was, for me, the perfect psychological moment. I had been playing with a story idea on a subject I had always suspected I would get around to sooner or later: the electric chair. "Old Sparky" has fascinated me ever since my first James Cagney movie, and the first Death Row tales I ever read (in a book called *Twenty Thousand Years in Sing Sing*, written by Warden Lewis E. Lawes) fired the darker side of my imagination. What, I wondered, would it be like to walk those last forty yards to the electric chair, knowing you were going to die there? What, for that matter, would it be like to be the man who had to strap the condemned in ... or pull the switch? What would such a job take out of you? Even creepier, what might it add?

I had tried these basic ideas, always tentatively, on a number of different frameworks over the last twenty or thirty years. I had written one successful novella set in prison (*Rita Hayworth and Shawshank Redemption*), and had sort of come to the conclusion that that was probably it for me, when this take on the idea came along. There were lots of things I liked about it, but nothing more than the narrator's essentially decent voice; low-key, honest, perhaps a little wide-eyed, he is a Stephen King narrator if ever there was one. So I got to work, but in a tentative, stop-and-start way. Most of the second chapter was written during a rain delay at Fenway Park!

When Ralph called, I had filled a notebook with scribbled pages of *The Green Mile,* and realized I was building a novel when I should have been spending my time clearing my desk for revisions on a book already written (*Desperation*—you'll see it soon, Constant Reader). At the point I had come to on *Mile,* there are usually just two choices: put it away (probably never to be picked up again) or cast everything else aside and chase.

Ralph suggested a possible third alternative, a story that could be written the same way it would be read—in installments. And I liked the high-wire aspect of it, too: fall down on the job, fail to carry through, and all at once about a million readers are howling for your blood. No one knows this any better than me, unless it's my secretary, Juliann Eugley; we get dozens of angry letters each week, demanding the next book in the *Dark Tower* cycle (patience, followers of Roland; another year or so and your wait will end, I promise). One of these contained a

Polaroid of a teddy-bear in chains, with a message cut out of newspaper headlines and magazine covers: RELEASE THE NEXT *DARK TOWER* BOOK AT ONCE OR THE BEAR DIES, it said. I put it up in my office to remind myself both of my responsibility and of how wonderful it is to have people actually care—a little—about the creatures of one's imagination.

In any case, I've decided to publish *The Green Mile* in a series of small paperbacks, in the nineteenth-century manner, and I hope you'll write and tell me (a) if you liked the story, and (b) if you liked the seldom used but rather amusing delivery system. It has certainly energized the writing of the story, although at this moment (a rainy evening in October of 1995) it is still far from done, even in rough draft, and the outcome remains in some doubt. That is part of the excitement of the whole thing, though—at this point I'm driving through thick fog with the pedal all the way to the metal.

Most of all, I want to say that if you have even half as much fun reading this as I did writing it, we'll both be well off. Enjoy . . . and why not read this aloud, with a friend? If nothing else, it will shorten the time until the next installment appears on your newsstand or in your local bookstore.

In the meantime, take care, and be good to one another.

—Stephen King

The Green Mile

Part One:
The Two Dead Girls

1

This happened in 1932, when the state penitentiary was still at Cold Mountain. And the electric chair was there, too, of course.

The inmates made jokes about the chair the way people always make jokes about things that frighten them but can't be gotten away from. They called it Old Sparky, or the Big Juicy. They made cracks about the power bill, and how Warden Moores would cook his Thanksgiving dinner that fall, with his wife, Melinda, too sick to cook.

But for the ones who actually had to sit down in that chair, the humor went out of the situation in a hurry. I presided over seventy-eight executions during my time at Cold Mountain (that's one figure I've never been confused about; I'll remember it on my deathbed), and I think that, for most of these men, the truth of what was happening to them finally hit all the way home when their ankles were being clamped to the stout oak of "Old Sparky's" legs. The realization came then (you would see it rising in their eyes, a kind of cold dismay) that their own legs had finished their careers. The blood still ran in them, the muscles were still strong, but they were finished, all the same; they were never going to walk another country mile or dance with a girl at a barn-raising. Old Sparky's clients came to a knowledge of their deaths from the ankles up. There was a black silk bag that went over their heads after they had finished their rambling and mostly disjointed last remarks. It was supposed to be for them, but I always thought it was really for us, to keep us from seeing the awful tide of dismay in their eyes as they realized they were going to die with their knees bent.

There was no death row at Cold Mountain, only E Block, set apart from the other four and about a quarter their size, brick instead of wood, with a horrible bare metal roof that glared in the summer sun like a delirious eyeball. Six cells inside, three on each side of a wide center aisle, each almost twice as big as the cells in the other four blocks. Singles, too. Great accommodations for a prison (especially in the thirties), but the inmates would have traded for cells in any of the other four. Believe me, they would have traded.

There was never a time during my years as block superintendent when all six cells were occupied at one time—thank God for small favors. Four was the most, mixed black and white (at Cold Mountain, there was no segregation among the walking dead), and that was a little piece of hell. One was a woman, Beverly McCall. She was black as the ace of

1. THE TWO DEAD GIRLS

spades and as beautiful as the sin you never had nerve enough to commit. She put up with six years of her husband beating her, but wouldn't put up with his creeping around for a single day. On the evening after she found out he was cheating, she stood waiting for the unfortunate Lester McCall, known to his pals (and, presumably, to his extremely short-term mistress) as Cutter, at the top of the stairs leading to the apartment over his barber shop. She waited until he got his overcoat half off, then dropped his cheating guts onto his tu-tone shoes. Used one of Cutter's own razors to do it. Two nights before she was due to sit in Old Sparky, she called me to her cell and said she had been visited by her African spirit-father in a dream. He told her to discard her slave-name and to die under her free name, Matuomi. That was her request, that her death-warrant should be read under the name of Beverly Matuomi. I guess her spirit-father didn't give her any first name, or one she could make out, anyhow. I said yes, okay, fine. One thing those years serving as the bull-goose screw taught me was never to refuse the condemned unless I absolutely had to. In the case of Beverly Matuomi, it made no difference, anyway. The governor called the next day around three in the afternoon, commuting her sentence to life in the Grassy Valley Penal Facility for Women—all penal and no penis, we used to say back then. I was glad to see Bev's round ass going left instead of right when she got to the duty desk, let me tell you.

Thirty-five years or so later—had to be at least thirty-five—I saw that name on the obituary page of the paper, under a picture of a skinny-faced black lady with a cloud of white hair and glasses with rhinestones at the corners. It was Beverly. She'd spent the last ten years of her life a free woman, the obituary said, and had rescued the small-town library of Raines Falls pretty much single-handed. She had also taught Sunday school and had been much loved in that little backwater. LIBRARIAN DIES OF HEART FAILURE, the headline said, and below that, in smaller type, almost as an afterthought: *Served Over Two Decades in Prison for Murder*. Only the eyes, wide and blazing behind the glasses with the rhinestones at the corners, were the same. They were the eyes of a woman who even at seventy-whatever would not hesitate to pluck a safety razor from its blue jar of disinfectant, if the urge seemed pressing. You know murderers, even if they finish up as old lady librarians in dozey little towns. At least you do if you've spent as much time minding murderers as I did. There was only one time I ever had a question about the nature of my job. That, I reckon, is why I'm writing this.

The wide corridor up the center of E Block was floored with linoleum the color of tired old limes, and so what was called the Last Mile at other prisons was called the Green Mile at Cold Mountain. It ran, I guess, sixty long paces from south to north, bottom to top. At the bottom was the restraint room. At the top end was a T-junction. A left turn meant life—if you called what went on in the sunbaked exercise yard life, and many did; many lived it for years, with no apparent ill effects. Thieves and arsonists and sex criminals, all talking their talk and walking their walk and making their little deals.

A right turn, though—that was different. First you went into my office (where the carpet was a so green, a thing I kept meaning to change and not getting around to), and crossed in front of my desk, which was flanked by the American flag on the left and the state flag on the right. On the far side were two doors. One led into the small W.C. that I and the Block E guards (sometimes even Warden Moores) used; the other opened on a kind of storage shed. This was where you ended up when you walked the Green Mile.

It was a small door—I had to duck my head when I went through, and John Coffey actually had to sit and scoot. You came out on a little landing, then went down three cement steps to a board floor. It was a miserable room without heat and with a metal roof, just like the one on the block to which it was an adjunct. It was cold enough in there to see your breath during the winter, and stifling in the summer. At the execution of Elmer Manfred—in July or August of '30, that one was, I believe—we had nine witnesses pass out.

On the left side of the storage shed—again—there was life. Tools (all locked down in frames crisscrossed with chains, as if they were carbine rifles instead of spades and pickaxes), dry goods, sacks of seeds for spring planting in the prison gardens, boxes of toilet paper, pallets cross-loaded with blanks for the prison plate-shop . . . even bags of lime for marking out the baseball diamond and the football gridiron—the cons played in what was known as The Pasture, and fall afternoons were greatly looked forward to at Cold Mountain.

On the right—once again—death. Old Sparky his ownself, sitting up on a plank platform at the southeast corner of the store room, stout oak legs, broad oak arms that had absorbed the terrorized sweat of scores of men in the last few minutes of their lives, and the metal cap, usually hung jauntily on the back of the chair, like some robot kid's beanie in a Buck Rogers comic-strip. A cord ran from it and through a gasket-circled hole in the cinderblock wall behind the chair. Off to one side was a galvanized tin bucket. If you looked inside it, you would see a circle of sponge, cut just right to fit the metal cap. Before executions, it was soaked in brine to better conduct the charge of direct-current electricity that ran through the wire, through the sponge, and into the condemned man's brain.

2

1932 was the year of John Coffey. The details would be in the papers, still there for anyone who cared enough to look them out—someone with more energy than one very old man whittling away the end of his life in a Georgia nursing home. That was a hot fall, I remember that; very hot, indeed October almost like August, and the warden's wife, Melinda, up in the hospital at Indianola for a spell. It was the fall I had the worst urinary infection of my life, not bad enough to put me in the hospital myself, but almost bad enough for me to wish I was dead every time I took a leak. It was the fall of Delacroix, the little half-bald Frenchman with the mouse, the one that came in the summer and did that cute trick with the spool. Mostly, though, it was the fall that John Coffey came to E Block, sentenced to death for the rape-murder of the Detterick twins.

There were four or five guards on the block each shift, but a lot of them were floaters. Dean Stanton, Harry Terwilliger, and Brutus Howell (the men called him "Brutal," but it was a joke, he wouldn't hurt a fly unless he had to, in spite of his size) are all dead now, and so is Percy Wetmore, who really *was* brutal . . . not to mention stupid. Percy had no business on E Block, where an ugly nature was useless and sometimes dangerous, but he was related to the governor by marriage, and so he stayed.

It was Percy Wetmore who ushered Coffey onto the block, with the supposedly traditional cry of "Dead man walking! Dead man walking here!"

It was still as hot as the hinges of hell, October or not. The door to the exercise yard opened, letting in a flood of brilliant light and the biggest man I've ever seen, except for some of the basketball fellows they have on the TV down in the "Resource Room" of this home for wayward droolers I've finished up in. He wore chains on his arms and across his water-barrel of a chest; he wore legirons on his ankles and shuffled a chain between them that sounded like cascading coins as it ran along the lime-colored corridor between the cells. Percy Wetmore was on one side of him, skinny little Harry Terwilliger was on the other, and they looked like children walking along with a captured bear. Even Brutus Howell looked like a kid next to Coffey, and Brutal was over six feet tall and broad as well, a football tackle who had gone on to play at LSU until he flunked out and came back home to the ridges.

John Coffey was black, like most of the men who came to stay for awhile in E Block before dying in

Old Sparky's lap, and he stood six feet, eight inches tall. He wasn't all willowy like the TV basketball fellows, though—he was broad in the shoulders and deep through the chest, laced over with muscle in every direction. They'd put him in the biggest denims they could find in Stores, and still the cuffs of the pants rode halfway up on his bunched and scarred calves. The shirt was open to below his chest, and the sleeves stopped somewhere on his forearms. He was holding his cap in one huge hand, which was just as well; perched on his bald mahogany ball of a head, it would have looked like the kind of cap an organ-grinder's monkey wears, only blue instead of red. He looked like he could have snapped the chains that held him as easily as you might snap the ribbons on a Christmas present, but when you looked in his face, you knew he wasn't going to do anything like that. It wasn't dull—although that was what Percy thought, it wasn't long before Percy was calling him the ijit—but *lost*. He kept looking around as if to make out where he was. Maybe even *who* he was. My first thought was that he looked like a black Samson . . . only after Delilah had shaved him smooth as her faithless little hand and taken all the fun out of him.

"Dead man walking!" Percy trumpeted, hauling on that bear of a man's wristcuff, as if he really believed he could move him if Coffey decided he didn't want to move anymore on his own. Harry didn't say anything, but he looked embarrassed. "Dead man—"

"That'll be enough of that," I said. I was in what

was going to be Coffey's cell, sitting on his bunk. I'd known he was coming, of course, was there to welcome him and take charge of him, but had no idea of the man's pure size until I saw him. Percy gave me a look that said we all knew I was an asshole (except for the big dummy, of course, who only knew how to rape and murder little girls), but he didn't say anything.

The three of them stopped outside the cell door, which was standing open on its track. I nodded to Harry, who said: "Are you sure you want to be in there with him, boss?" I didn't often hear Harry Terwilliger sound nervous—he'd been right there by my side during the riots of six or seven years before and had never wavered, even when the rumors that some of them had guns began to circulate—but he sounded nervous then.

"Am I going to have any trouble with you, big boy?" I asked, sitting there on the bunk and trying not to look or sound as miserable as I felt—that urinary infection I mentioned earlier wasn't as bad as it eventually got, but it was no day at the beach, let me tell you.

Coffey shook his head slowly—once to the left, once to the right, then back to dead center. Once his eyes found me, they never left me.

Harry had a clipboard with Coffey's forms on it in one hand. "Give it to him," I said to Harry. "Put it in his hand."

Harry did. The big mutt took it like a sleepwalker.

"Now bring it to me, big boy," I said, and Coffey did, his chains jingling and rattling. He had to duck his head just to enter the cell.

I looked up and down mostly to register his height as a fact and not an optical illusion. It was real: six feet, eight inches. His weight was given as two-eighty, but I think that was only an estimate; he had to have been three hundred and twenty, maybe as much as three hundred and fifty pounds. Under the space for scars and identifying marks, one word had been blocked out in the laborious printing of Magnusson, the old trusty in Registration: *Numerous.*

I looked up. Coffey had shuffled a bit to one side and I could see Harry standing across the corridor in front of Delacroix's cell—he was our only other prisoner in E Block when Coffey came in. Del was a slight, balding man with the worried face of an accountant who knows his embezzlement will soon be discovered. His tame mouse was sitting on his shoulder.

Percy Wetmore was leaning in the doorway of the cell which had just become John Coffey's. He had taken his hickory baton out of the custom-made holster he carried it in, and was tapping it against one palm the way a man does when he has a toy he wants to use. And all at once I couldn't stand to have him there. Maybe it was the unseasonable heat, maybe it was the urinary infection heating up my groin and making the itch of my flannel underwear all but unbearable, maybe it was knowing that the state had sent me a black man next door to an idiot to execute, and Percy clearly wanted to hand-tool him a little first. Probably it was all those things. Whatever it was, I stopped caring about his political connections for a little while.

"Percy," I said. "They're moving house over in the infirmary."

"Bill Dodge is in charge of that detail—"

"I know he is," I said. "Go and help him."

"That isn't my job," Percy said. "This big lugoon is my job." "Lugoon" was Percy's joke name for the big ones—a combination of *lug* and *goon*. He resented the big ones. He wasn't skinny, like Harry Terwilliger, but he was short. A banty-rooster sort of guy, the kind that likes to pick fights, especially when the odds are all their way. And vain about his hair. Could hardly keep his hands off it.

"Then your job is done," I said. "Get over to the infirmary."

His lower lip pooched out. Bill Dodge and his men were moving boxes and stacks of sheets, even the beds; the whole infirmary was going to a new frame building over on the west side of the prison. Hot work, heavy lifting. Percy Wetmore wanted no part of either.

"They got all the men they need," he said.

"Then get over there and straw-boss," I said, raising my voice. I saw Harry wince and paid no attention. If the governor ordered Warden Moores to fire me for ruffling the wrong set of feathers, who was

Hal Moores going to put in my place? Percy? It was a joke. "I really don't care what you do. Percy, as long as you get out of here for awhile."

For a moment I thought he was going to stick and there'd be real trouble, with Coffey standing there the whole time like the world's biggest stopped clock. Then Percy rammed his billy back into its hand-tooled holster—foolish damned vanitorious thing—and went stalking up the corridor. I don't remember which guard was sitting at the duty desk that day—one of the floaters, I guess—but Percy must not have liked the way he looked, because he growled, "You wipe that smirk off your shitepoke face or I'll wipe it off for you" as he went by. There was a rattle of keys, a momentary blast of hot sunlight from the exercise yard, and then Percy Wetmore was gone, at least for the time being. Delacroix's mouse ran back and forth from one of the little Frenchman's shoulders to the other, his filament whiskers twitching.

"Be still, Mr. Jingles," Delacroix said, and the mouse stopped on his left shoulder just as if he had understood. "Just be so still and so quiet." In Delacroix's lilting Cajun accent, *quiet* came out sounding exotic and foreign—*kwaht.*

"You go lie down, Del," I said curtly. "Take you a rest. This is none of your business, either."

He did as I said. He had raped a young girl and killed her, and had then dropped her body behind the apartment house where she lived, doused it with coal-oil, and then set it on fire, hoping in some muddled way to dispose of the evidence of his crime. The fire had spread to the building itself, had engulfed it, and six more people had died, two of them children. It was the only crime he had in him, and now he was just a mild-mannered man with a worried face, a bald pate, and long hair straggling over the back of his shirt-collar. He would sit down with Old Sparky in a little while, and Old Sparky would make an end to him ... but whatever it was that had done that awful thing was already gone, and now he lay on his bunk, letting his little companion run squeaking over his hands. In a way, that was the worst; Old Sparky never burned what was inside them, and the drugs they inject them with today don't put it to sleep. It vacates, jumps to someone else, and leaves us to kill husks that aren't really alive anyway.

I turned my attention to the giant.

"If I let Harry take those chains off you, are you going to be nice?"

He nodded. It was like his head-shake: down, up, back to center. His strange eyes looked at me. There was a kind of peace in them, but not a kind I was sure I could trust. I crooked a finger to Harry, who came in and unlocked the chains. He showed no fear now, even when he knelt between Coffey's treetrunk legs to unlock the ankle irons, and that eased me some. It was Percy who had made Harry nervous, and I trusted Harry's instincts. I trusted the instincts of all my day-to-day E Block men, except for Percy.

I have a little set speech I make to men new on the block, but I hesitated with Coffey, because he seemed so abnormal, and not just in his size.

When Harry stood back (Coffey had remained motionless during the entire unlocking ceremony, as placid as a Percheron), I looked up at my new charge, tapping on the clipboard with my thumb, and said: "Can you talk, big boy?"

"Yes, sir, boss, I can talk," he said. His voice was a deep and quiet rumble. It made me think of a freshly tuned tractor engine. He had no real Southern drawl—he said *I*, not *Ah*—but there was a kind of Southern construction to his speech that I noticed later. As if he was *from* the South, but not *of* it. He didn't sound illiterate, but he didn't sound educated. In his speech as in so many other things, he was a mystery. Mostly it was his eyes that troubled me—a kind of peaceful absence in them, as if he were floating far, far away.

"Your name is John Coffey."

"Yes, sir, boss, like the drink, only not spelled the same way."

"So you can spell, can you? Read and write?"

"Just my name, boss," said he, serenely.

I sighed, then gave him a short version of my set speech. I'd already decided he wasn't going to be any trouble. In that I was both right and wrong.

"My name is Paul Edgecombe," I said. "I'm the E Block super—the head screw. You want something from me, ask for me by name. If I'm not here, ask this other man—his name is Harry Terwilliger. Or you ask for Mr. Stanton or Mr. Howell. Do you understand that?"

Coffey nodded.

"Just don't expect to get what you want unless we decide it's what you need—this isn't a hotel. Still with me?"

He nodded again.

"This is a quiet place, big boy—not like the rest of the prison. It's just you and Delacroix over there. You won't work; mostly you'll just sit. Give you a chance to think things over." Too much time for most of them, but I didn't say that. "Sometimes we play the radio, if all's in order. You like the radio?"

He nodded, but doubtfully, as if he wasn't sure what the radio was. I later found out that was true, in a way; Coffey knew things when he encountered them again, but in between he forgot. He knew the characters on *Our Gal Sunday*, but had only the haziest memory of what they'd been up to the last time.

"If you behave, you'll eat on time, you'll never see the solitary cell down at the far end, or have to wear one of those canvas coats that buttons up the back. You'll have two hours in the yard afternoons from four until six, except on Saturdays when the rest of the prison population has their flag football games. You'll have your visitors on Sunday afternoons, if you have someone who wants to visit you. Do you, Coffey?"

He shook his head. "Got none, boss," he said.

"Well, your lawyer, then."

"I believe I've seen the back end of him," he said. "He was give to me on loan. Don't believe he could find his way up here in the mountains."

I looked at him closely to see if he might be trying a little joke, but he didn't seem to be. And I really hadn't expected any different. Appeals weren't for the likes of John Coffey, not back then; they had their day in court and then the world forgot them until they saw a squib in the paper saying a certain fellow had taken a little electricity along about midnight. But a man with a wife, children, or friends to look forward to on Sunday afternoons was easier to control, if control looked to be a problem. Here it didn't, and that was good. Because he was so damned big.

I shifted a little on the bunk, then decided I might feel a little more comfortable in my nether parts if I stood up, and so I did. He backed away from me respectfully, and clasped his hands in front of him.

"Your time here can be easy or hard, big boy, it all depends on you. I'm here to say you might as well make it easy on all of us, because it comes to the same in the end. We'll treat you as right as you deserve. Do you have any questions?"

"Do you leave a light on after bedtime?" he asked right away, as if he had only been waiting for the chance.

I blinked at him. I had been asked a lot of strange

questions by newcomers to E Block—once about the size of my wife's tits—but never that one.

Coffey was smiling a trifle uneasily, as if he knew we would think him foolish but couldn't help himself. "Because I get a little scared in the dark sometimes," he said. "If it's a strange place."

I looked at him—the pure size of him—and felt strangely touched. They did touch you, you know; you didn't see them at their worst, hammering out their horrors like demons at a forge.

"Yes, it's pretty bright in here all night long," I said. "Half the lights along the Mile burn from nine until five every morning." Then I realized he wouldn't have any idea of what I was talking about—he didn't know the Green Mile from Mississippi mud—and so I pointed. "In the corridor."

He nodded, relieved. I'm not sure he knew what a corridor was, either, but he could see the 200-watt bulbs in their wire cages.

I did something I'd never done to a prisoner before, then—I offered him my hand. Even now I don't know why. Him asking about the lights, maybe. It made Harry Terwilliger blink, I can tell you that. Coffey took my hand with surprising gentleness, my hand all but disappearing into his, and that was all of it. I had another moth in my killing bottle. We were done.

I stepped out of the cell. Harry pulled the door shut on its track and ran both locks. Coffey stood where he was a moment or two longer, as if he didn't know what to do next, and then he sat down on his bunk, clasped his giant's hands between his knees, and lowered his head like a man who grieves or prays. He said something then in his strange, almost-Southern voice. I heard it with perfect clarity, and although I didn't know much about what he'd done then—you don't need to know about what a man's done in order to feed him and groom him until it's time for him to pay off what he owes—it still gave me a chill.

"I couldn't help it, boss," he said. "I tried to take it back, but it was too late."

3

"You're going to have you some trouble with Percy," Harry said as we walked back up the hall and into my office. Dean Stanton, sort of my third in command—we didn't actually have such things, a situation Percy Wetmore would have fixed up in a flash—was sitting behind my desk, updating the files, a job I never seemed to get around to. He barely looked up as we came in, just gave his little glasses a shove with the ball of his thumb and dived back into his paperwork.

"I been having trouble with that peckerwood since the day he came here," I said, gingerly, pulling my pants away from my crotch and wincing. "Did you hear what he was shouting when he brought that big galoot down?"

"Couldn't very well not," Harry said. "I was there, you know."

"I was in the john and heard it just fine," Dean said. He drew a sheet of paper to him, held it up into the light so I could see there was a coffee-ring as well as typing on it, and then tossed it into the waste basket. " 'Dead man walking.' Must have read that in one of those magazines he likes so much."

And he probably had. Percy Wetmore was a great reader of *Argosy* and *Stag* and *Men's Adventure*. There was a prison tale in every issue, it seemed, and Percy read them avidly, like a man doing research. It was like he was trying to find out how to act, and thought the information was in those magazines. He'd come just after we did Anthony Ray, the hatchet-killer—and he hadn't actually participated in an execution yet, although he'd witnessed one from the switch-room.

"He knows people," Harry said. "He's connected. You'll have to answer for sending him off the block, and you'll have to answer even harder for expecting him to do some real work."

"I don't expect it," I said, and I didn't . . . but I had hopes. Bill Dodge wasn't the sort to let a man just stand around and do the heavy looking-on. "I'm more interested in the big boy, for the time being. Are we going to have trouble with him?"

Harry shook his head with decision.

"He was quiet as a lamb at court down there in Trapingus County," Dean said. He took his little rimless glasses off and began to polish them on his vest. "Of course they had more chains on him than Scrooge saw on Marley's ghost, but he could have kicked up dickens if he'd wanted. That's a pun, son."

"I know," I said, although I didn't. I just hate letting Dean Stanton get the better of me.

"Big one, ain't he?" Dean said.

"He is," I agreed. "Monstrous big."

"Probably have to crank Old Sparky up to Super Bake to fry his ass."

"Don't worry about Old Sparky," I said absently. "He makes the big 'uns little."

Dean pinched the sides of his nose, where there were a couple of angry red patches from his glasses, and nodded. "Yep," he said. "Some truth to that, all right."

I asked, "Do either of you know where he came from before he showed up in . . . Tefton? It was Tefton, wasn't it?"

"Yep," Dean said. "Tefton, down in Trapingus County. Before he showed up there and did what he did, no one seems to know. He just drifted around, I guess. You might be able to find out a little more from the newspapers in the prison library, if you're really interested. They probably won't get around to moving those until next week." He grinned. "You might have to listen to your little buddy bitching and moaning upstairs, though."

"I might just go have a peek, anyway," I said, and later on that afternoon I did.

The prison library was in back of the building that was going to become the prison auto shop—at least that was the plan. More pork in someone's pocket was what I thought, but the Depression was on, and

1. THE TWO DEAD GIRLS

I kept my opinions to myself—the way I should have kept my mouth shut about Percy, but sometimes a man just can't keep it clapped tight. A man's mouth gets him in more trouble than his pecker ever could, most of the time. And the auto shop never happened, anyway—the next spring, the prison moved sixty miles down the road to Brighton. More backroom deals, I reckon. More barrels of pork. Wasn't nothing to me.

Administration had gone to a new building on the east side of the yard; the infirmary was being moved (whose country-bumpkin idea it had been to put an infirmary on the second floor in the first place was just another of life's mysteries); the library was still partly stocked—not that it ever had much in it—and standing empty. The old building was a hot clapboard box kind of shouldered in between A and B Blocks. Their bathrooms backed up on it and the whole building was always swimming with this vague pissy smell, which was probably the only good reason for the move. The library was L-shaped, and not much bigger than my office. I looked for a fan, but they were all gone. It must have been a hundred degrees in there, and I could feel that hot throb in my groin when I sat down. Sort of like an infected tooth. I know that's absurd, considering the region we're talking about here, but it's the only thing I could compare it to. It got a lot worse during and just after taking a leak, which I had done just before walking over.

There was one other fellow there after all—a scrawny old trusty named Gibbons dozing away in the corner with a Wild West novel in his lap and his hat pulled down over his eyes. The heat wasn't bothering him, nor were the grunts, thumps, and occasional curses from the infirmary upstairs (where it had to be at least ten degrees hotter, and I hoped Percy Wetmore was enjoying it). I didn't bother him, either, but went around to the short side of the L, where the newspapers were kept. I thought they might be gone along with the fans, in spite of what Dean had said. They weren't, though, and the business about the Detterick twins was easily enough looked out; it had been front-page news from the commission of the crime in June right through the trial in late August and September.

Soon I had forgotten the heat and the thumps from upstairs and old Gibbons's wheezy snores. The thought of those little nine-year-old girls—their fluffy heads of blonde hair and their engaging Bobbsey Twins smiles—in connection with Coffey's hulking darkness was unpleasant but impossible to ignore. Given his size, it was easy to imagine him actually eating them, like a giant in a fairy tale. What he *had* done was even worse, and it was a lucky thing for him that he hadn't just been lynched right there on the riverbank. If, that was, you considered waiting to walk the Green Mile and sit in Old Sparky's lap lucky.

4

King Cotton had been deposed in the South seventy years before all these things happened and would never be king again, but in those years of the thirties it had a little revival. There were no more cotton plantations, but there were forty or fifty prosperous cotton farms in the southern part of our state. Klaus Detterick owned one of them. By the standards of the nineteen-fifties he would have been considered only a rung above shirttail poor, but by those of the thirties he was considered well-to-do because he actually paid his store bill in cash at the end of most months, and he could meet the bank president's eyes if they happened to pass on the street. The farmhouse was clean and commodious. In addition to the cotton, there were the other two c's: chickens and a few cows. He and his wife had three children: Howard, who was twelve or thereabouts, and the twin girls, Cora and Kathe.

On a warm night in June of that year, the girls asked for and were given permission to sleep on the screen-enclosed side porch, which ran the length of the house. This was a great treat for them. Their mother kissed them goodnight just shy of nine, when the last light had gone out of the sky. It was the final time she saw either of them until they were in their coffins and the undertaker had repaired the worst of the damage.

Country families went to bed early in those days— "soon as 'twas dark under the table," my own mother sometimes said—and slept soundly. Certainly Klaus, Marjorie, and Howie Detterick did on the night the twins were taken. Klaus would almost certainly have been wakened by Bowser, the family's big old half-breed collie, if he had barked, but Bowser didn't. Not that night, not ever again.

Klaus was up at first light to do the milking. The porch was on the side of the house away from the barn, and Klaus never thought to look in on the girls. Bowser's failure to join him was no cause for alarm, either. The dog held the cows and the chickens alike in great disdain, and usually hid in his doghouse behind the barn when the chores were being performed, unless called . . . and called energetically, at that.

Marjorie came downstairs fifteen minutes or so after her husband had pulled on his boots in the mudroom and tromped out to the barn. She started the coffee, then put bacon on to fry. The combined smells brought Howie down from his room under the eaves, but not the girls from the porch. She sent

Howie out to fetch them as she cracked eggs into the bacon grease. Klaus would want the girls out to get fresh ones as soon as breakfast was over. Except no breakfast was eaten in the Detterick house that morning. Howie came back from the porch, white around the gills and with his formerly sleep-puffy eyes now wide open.

"They're gone," he said.

Marjorie went out onto the porch, at first more annoyed than alarmed. She said later that she had supposed, if she had supposed anything, that the girls had decided to take a walk and pick flowers by the dawn's early light. That or some similar green-girl foolishness. One look, and she understood why Howie had been white.

She screamed for Klaus—*shrieked* for him—and Klaus came on the dead run, his workboots whitened by the half-full pail of milk he had spilled on them. What he found on the porch would have jellied the legs of the most courageous parent. The blankets in which the girls would have bundled themselves as the night drew on and grew colder had been cast into one corner. The screen door had been yanked off its upper hinge and hung drunkenly out into the dooryard. And on the boards of both the porch and the steps beyond the mutilated screen door, there were spatters of blood.

Marjorie begged her husband not to go hunting after the girls alone, and not to take their son if he felt he had to go after them, but she could have saved her breath. He took the shotgun he kept mounted in the mudroom high out of the reach of little hands, and gave Howie the .22 they had been saving for his birthday in July. Then they went, neither of them paying the slightest attention to the shrieking, weeping woman who wanted to know what they would do if they met a gang of wandering hobos or a bunch of bad niggers escaped from the county farm over in Laduc. In this I think the men were right, you know. The blood was no longer runny, but it was only tacky yet, and still closer to true red than the maroon that comes when blood has well dried. The abduction hadn't happened too long ago. Klaus must have reasoned that there was still a chance for his girls, and he meant to take it.

Neither one of them could track worth a damn—they were gatherers, not hunters, men who went into the woods after coon and deer in their seasons not because they much wanted to, but because it was an expected thing. And the dooryard around the house was a blighted patch of dirt with tracks all overlaid in a meaningless tangle. They went around the barn, and saw almost at once why Bowser, a bad biter but a good barker, hadn't sounded the alarm. He lay half in and half out of a doghouse which had been built of leftover barnboards (there was a signboard with the word *Bowser* neatly printed on it over the curved hole in the front—I saw a photograph of it in one of the papers), his head turned most of the way around on his neck. It would have taken a man of enormous power to have done that to such a big animal, the prosecutor later told John Coffey's jury ... and then he had looked long and meaningfully at the hulking defendant, sitting behind the defense table with his eyes cast down and wearing a brand-new pair of state-bought bib overalls that looked like damnation in and of themselves. Beside the dog, Klaus and Howie found a scrap of cooked link sausage. The theory—a sound one, I have no doubt—was that Coffey had first charmed the dog with treats, and then, as Bowser began to eat the last one, had reached out his hands and broken its neck with one mighty snap of his wrists.

Beyond the barn was Detterick's north pasture, where no cows would graze that day. It was drenched with morning dew, and leading off through it, cutting on a diagonal to the northwest and plain as day, was the beaten track of a man's passage.

Even in his state of near-hysteria, Klaus Detterick hesitated at first to follow it. It wasn't fear of the man or men who had taken his daughters; it was fear of following the abductor's backtrail ... of going off in exactly the wrong direction at a time when every second might count.

Howie solved that dilemma by plucking a shred of yellow cotton cloth from a bush growing just beyond the edge of the dooryard. Klaus was shown this same scrap of cloth as he sat on the witness stand, and began to weep as he identified it as a piece of his daughter Kathe's sleeping-shorts. Twenty yards beyond it, hanging from the jutting finger of a juniper shrub, they found a piece of faded green cloth that matched the nightie Cora had been wearing when she kissed her ma and pa goodnight.

The Dettericks, father and son, set off at a near-run with their guns held in front of them, as soldiers do when crossing contested ground under heavy fire. If I wonder at anything that happened that day, it is that the boy, chasing desperately after his father (and often in danger of being left behind completely), never fell and put a bullet in Klaus Detterick's back.

The farmhouse was on the exchange—another sign to the neighbors that the Dettericks were prospering, at least moderately, in disastrous times—and Marjorie used Central to call as many of her neighbors that were also on the exchange as she could, telling them of the disaster which had fallen like a lightning-stroke out of a clear sky, knowing that each call would produce overlapping ripples, like pebbles tossed rapidly into a stilly pond. Then she lifted the handset one last time, and spoke those words that were almost a trademark of the early telephone systems of that time, at least in the rural South: "Hello, Central, are you on the line?"

Central was, but for a moment could say nothing; that worthy woman was all agog. At last she managed, "Yes, ma'am, Mrs. Detterick, I sure am, oh dear sweet blessed Jesus, I'm a-prayin right now that your little girls are all right—"

"Yes, thank you," Marjorie said. "But you tell the

Lord to wait long enough for you to put me through to the high sheriff's office down Tefton, all right?"

The Trapingus County high sheriff was a whiskey-nosed old boy with a gut like a washtub and a head of white hair so fine it looked like pipe-cleaner fuzz. I knew him well; he'd been up to Cold Mountain plenty of times to see what he called "his boys" off into the great beyond. Execution witnesses sat in the same folding chairs you've probably sat in yourself a time or two, at funerals or church suppers or Grange bingo (in fact, we borrowed ours from the Mystic Tie No. 44 Grange back in those days), and every time Sheriff Homer Cribus sat down in one, I waited for the dry crack that would signal collapse. I dreaded that day and hoped for it, both at the same time, but it was a day that never came. Not long after—couldn't have been more than one summer after the Detterick girls were abducted—he had a heart attack in his office, apparently while screwing a seventeen-year-old black girl named Daphne Shurtleff There was a lot of talk about that, with him always sporting his wife and six boys around so prominent come election time—those were the days when, if you wanted to run for something, the saying used to be "Be Baptist or be gone." But people love a hypocrite, you know—they recognize one of their own, and it always feels so good when someone gets caught with his pants down and his dick up and it isn't you.

Besides being a hypocrite, he was incompetent, the kind of fellow who'd get himself photographed petting some lady's cat when it was someone else— Deputy Rob McGee, for instance—who'd actually risked a broken collarbone by going up the tree where Mistress Pussycat was and bringing her down.

McGee listened to Marjorie Detterick babble for maybe two minutes, then cut her off with four or five questions—quick and curt, like a trained fighter's flicking little jabs to the face, the kind of punches that are so small and so hard that the blood comes before the sting. When he had answers to these, he said: "I'll call Bobo Marchant. He's got dogs. You stay put, Miz Detterick. If your man and your boy come back, make them stay put, too. Try, anyway."

Her man and her boy had, meanwhile, followed the track of the abductor three miles to the north-west, but when his trail ran out of open fields and into piney woods, they lost it. They were farmers, not hunters, as I have said, and by then they knew it was an animal they were after. Along the way they had found the yellow top that matched Kathe's shorts, and another piece of Cora's nightie. Both items were drenched with blood, and neither Klaus nor Howie was in as much of a hurry as they had been at the start; a certain cold certainty must have been filtering into their hot hopes by then, working its way down-ward the way cold water does, sinking because it is heavier.

They cast into the woods, looking for signs, found none, cast in a second place with similar lack of re-sult, then in a third. This time they found a fantail of blood splashed across the needles of a loblolly pine. They went in the direction it seemed to point for a little way, then began the casting-about process again. It was by then nine o'clock in the morning, and from behind them they began to hear shouting men and baying dogs. Rob McGee had put together a jackleg posse in the time it would have taken Sheriff Cribus to finish his first brandy-sweetened cup of coffee, and by quarter past the hour they reached Klaus and Howie Detterick, the two of them stumbling desperately around on the edge of the woods. Soon the men were moving again, with Bobo's dogs leading the way. McGee let Klaus and Howie go on with them—they wouldn't have gone back if he'd ordered them, no matter how much they dreaded the outcome, and McGee must have seen that—but he made them unload their weapons. The others had done the same, McGee said; it was safer. What he didn't tell them (nor did anyone else) was that the Dettericks were the only ones who had been asked to turn their loads over to the deputy. Half-distracted and wanting only to go through to the end of the nightmare and be done with it, they did as he asked. When Rob McGee got the Dettericks to unload their guns and give him their loads, he probably saved John Coffey's miserable excuse for a life.

The baying, yawping dogs pulled them through two miles of scrub pine, always on that same rough northwest heading. Then they came out on the edge of the Trapingus River, which is wide and slow at that point, running southeast through low, wooded hills where families named Cray and Robinette and Duplissey still made their own mandolins and often spat out their own rotted teeth as they plowed; deep countryside where men were apt to handle snakes on Sunday morning and lie down in carnal embrace with their daughters on Sunday night. I knew their families; most of them had sent Sparky a meal from time to time. On the far side of the river, the members of the posse could see the June sun glinting off the steel rails of a Great Southern branch line. About a mile downstream to their right, a trestle crossed toward the coal-fields of West Green.

Here they found a wide trampled patch in the grass and low bushes, a patch so bloody that many of the men had to sprint back into the woods and relieve themselves of their breakfasts. They also found the rest of Cora's nightgown lying in this bloody patch, and Howie, who had held up admirably until then, reeled back against his father and nearly fainted.

And it was here that Bobo Marchant's dogs had their first and only disagreement of the day. There were six in all, two bloodhounds, two bluetick hounds, and a couple of those terrierlike mongrels border Southerners call coon hounds. The coonies wanted to go northwest, upstream along the Trapingus; the rest wanted to go in the other direction, southeast. They got all tangled in their leads, and although the papers said nothing about this part,

I could imagine the horrible curses Bobo must have rained down on them as he used his hands—surely the most educated part of him—to get them straightened around again. I have known a few hound-dog men in my time, and it's been my experience that, as a class, they run remarkably true to type.

Bobo shortleashed them into a pack, then ran Cora Detterick's torn nightgown under their noses, to kind of remind them what they were doing out on a day when the temperature would be in the mid-nineties by noon and the noseeums were already circling the heads of the possemen in clouds. The coonies took another sniff, decided to vote the straight ticket, and off they all went downstream, in full cry.

It wasn't but ten minutes later when the men stopped, realizing they could hear more than just the dogs. It was a howling rather than a baying, and a sound no dog had ever made, not even in its dying extremities. It was a sound none of them had ever heard *anything* make, but they knew right away, all of them, that it was a man. So they said, and I believed them. I think I would have recognized it, too. I have heard men scream just that way, I think, on their way to the electric chair. Not a lot—most button themselves up and go either quiet or joking, like it was the class picnic—but a few. Usually the ones who believe in hell as a real place, and know it is waiting for them at the end of the Green Mile.

Bobo shortleashed his dogs again. They were valuable, and he had no intention of losing them to the psychopath howling and gibbering just down yonder. The other men reloaded their guns and snapped them closed. That howling had chilled them all, and made the sweat under their arms and running down their backs feel like icewater. When men take a chill like that, they need a leader if they are to go on, and Deputy McGee led them. He got out in front and walked briskly (I bet he didn't *feel* very brisk right then, though) to a stand of alders that jutted out of the woods on the right, with the rest of them trundling along nervously about five paces behind. He paused just once, and that was to motion the biggest man among them—Sam Hollis—to keep near Klaus Detterick.

On the other side of the alders there was more open ground stretching back to the woods on the right. On the left was the long, gentle slope of the riverbank. They all stopped where they were, thunderstruck. I think they would have given a good deal to unsee what was before them, and none of them would ever forget it—it was the sort of nightmare, bald and almost smoking in the sun, that lies beyond the drapes and furnishings of good and ordinary lives—church suppers, walks along country lanes, honest work, love-kisses in bed. There is a skull in every man, and I tell you there is a skull in the lives of all men. They saw it that day, those men—they saw what sometimes grins behind the smile.

Sitting on the riverbank in a faded, bloodstained jumper was the biggest man any of them had ever seen—John Coffey. His enormous, splay-toed feet were bare. On his head he wore a faded red bandanna, the way a country woman would wear a kerchief into church. Gnats circled him in a black cloud. Curled in each arm was the body of a naked girl. Their blonde hair, once curly and light as milkweed fluff, was now matted to their heads and streaked red. The man holding them sat bawling up at the sky like a moonstruck calf, his dark brown cheeks slicked with tears, his face twisted in a monstrous cramp of grief. He drew breath in hitches, his chest rising until the snaps holding the straps of his jumper were strained, and then let that vast catch of air out in another of those howls. So often you read in the paper that "the killer showed no remorse," but that wasn't the case here. John Coffey was torn open by what he had done . . . but he would live. The girls would not. They had been torn open in a more fundamental way.

No one seemed to know how long they stood there, looking at the howling man who was, in his turn, looking across the great still plate of the river at a train on the other side, storming down the tracks toward the trestle that crossed the river. It seemed they looked for an hour or for forever, and yet the train got no farther along, it seemed to storm only in one place, like a child doing a tantrum, and the sun did not go behind a cloud, and the sight was not blotted from their eyes. It was there before them, as real as a dogbite. The black man rocked back and forth; Cora and Kathe rocked with him like dolls in the arms of a giant. The bloodstained muscles in the man's huge, bare arms flexed and relaxed, flexed and relaxed, flexed and relaxed.

It was Klaus Detterick who broke the tableau. Screaming, he flung himself at the monster who had raped and killed his daughters. Sam Hollis knew his job and tried to do it, but couldn't. He was six inches taller than Klaus and outweighed him by at least seventy pounds, but Klaus seemed to almost shrug his encircling arms off. Klaus flew across the intervening open ground and launched a flying kick at Coffey's head. His workboot, caked with spilled milk that had already soured in the heat, scored a direct hit on Coffey's left temple, but Coffey seemed not to feel it at all. He only sat there, keening and rocking and looking out across the river; the way I imagine it, he could almost have been a picture out of some piney woods Pentecostal sermon, the faithful follower of the Cross looking out toward Goshen Land ... if not for the corpses, that was.

It took four men to haul the hysterical farmer off John Coffey, and he fetched Coffey I don't know how many good licks before they finally did. It didn't seem to matter to Coffey, one way or the other; he just went on looking out across the river and keening. As for Detterick, all the fight went out of him when he was finally pulled off—as if some strange galvanizing current had been running through the huge black man (I still have a tendency to think in electrical metaphors; you'll have to pardon me), and when Detterick's contact with that power source was finally broken, he went as limp as a man flung back from a live wire. He knelt wide-legged on the riverbank with his hands to his face, sobbing. Howie joined him and they hugged each other forehead to forehead.

Two men watched them while the rest formed a rifle-toting ring around the rocking, wailing black man. He still seemed not to realize that anyone but him was there. McGee stepped forward, shifted uncertainly from foot to foot for a bit, then hunkered.

"Mister," he said in a quiet voice, and Coffey hushed at once. McGee looked at eyes that were bloodshot from crying. And still they streamed, as if someone had left a faucet on inside him. Those eyes wept, and yet were somehow untouched . . . distant and serene. I thought them the strangest eyes I had ever seen in my life, and McGee felt much the same. "Like the eyes of an animal that never saw a man before," he told a reporter named Hammersmith just before the trial.

"Mister, do you hear me?" McGee asked.

Slowly, Coffey nodded his head. Still he curled his arms around his unspeakable dolls, their chins down on their chests so their faces could not be clearly seen, one of the few mercies God saw fit to bestow that day.

"Do you have a name?" McGee asked.

"John Coffey," he said in a thick and tear-clotted

voice. "Coffey like the drink, only not spelled the same way."

McGee nodded, then pointed a thumb at the chest pocket of Coffey's jumper, which was bulging. It looked to McGee like it might have been a gun—not that a man Coffey's size would need a gun to do some major damage, if he decided to go off. "What's that in there, John Coffey? Is that maybe a heater? A pistol?"

"Nosir," Coffey said in his thick voice, and those strange eyes—welling tears and agonized on top, distant and weirdly serene underneath, as if the true John Coffey was somewhere else, looking out on some other landscape where murdered little girls were nothing to get all worked up about—never left Deputy McGee's. "That's just a little lunch I have."

"Oh, now, a little lunch, is that right?" McGee asked, and Coffey nodded and said yessir with his eyes running and clear snot-runners hanging out of his nose. "And where did the likes of you get a little lunch, John Coffey?" Forcing himself to be calm, although he could smell the girls by then, and could see the flies lighting and sampling the places on them that were wet. It was their hair that was the worst, he said later . . . and this wasn't in any newspaper story; it was considered too grisly for family reading. No, this I got from the reporter who wrote the story, Mr. Hammersmith. I looked him up later on, because later on John Coffey became sort of an obsession with me. McGee told this Hammersmith that their blonde hair wasn't blonde anymore. It was auburn. Blood had run down their cheeks out of it like it was a bad dye-job, and you didn't have to be a doctor to see that their fragile skulls had been dashed together with the force of those mighty arms. Probably they had been crying. Probably he had wanted to make them stop. If the girls had been lucky, this had happened before the rapes.

Looking at that made it hard for a man to think, even a man as determined to do his job as Deputy McGee was. Bad thinking could cause mistakes, maybe more bloodshed. McGee drew him in a deep breath and calmed himself. Tried, anyway.

"Wellsir, I don't exactly remember, be dog if I do," Coffey said in his tear-choked voice, "but it's a little lunch, all right, sammidges and I think a swee' pickle."

"I might just have a look for myself, it's all the same to you," McGee said. "Don't you move now, John Coffey. Don't do it, boy, because there are enough guns aimed at you to make you disappear from the waist up should you so much as twitch a finger."

Coffey looked out across the river and didn't move as McGee gently reached into the chest pocket of those biballs and pulled out something wrapped in newspaper and tied with a hank of butcher's twine. McGee snapped the string and opened the paper, although he was pretty sure it was just what Coffey said it was, a little lunch. There was a bacon-tomato sandwich and a jelly fold-over. There was also a pickle, wrapped in its own piece of a funny page John Coffey would never be able to puzzle out. There were no sausages. Bowser had gotten the sausages out of John Coffey's little lunch.

McGee handed the lunch back over his shoulder to one of the other men without taking his eyes off Coffey. Hunkered down like that, he was too close to want to let his attention stray for even a second. The lunch, wrapped up again and tied for good measure, finally ended up with Bobo Marchant, who put it in his knapsack, where he kept treats for his dogs (and a few fishing lures, I shouldn't wonder). It wasn't introduced into evidence at the trial—justice in this part of the world is swift, but not as swift as a bacon-tomato sandwich goes over—though photographs of it were.

"What happened here, John Coffey?" McGee asked in his low, earnest voice. "You want to tell me that?"

And Coffey said to McGee and the others almost exactly the same thing he said to me; they were also the last words the prosecutor said to the jury at Coffey's trial. "I couldn't help it," John Coffey said, holding the murdered, violated girls naked in his arms. The tears began to pour down his cheeks again. "I tried to take it back, but it was too late."

"Boy, you are under arrest for murder," McGee said, and then he spit in John Coffey's face.

The jury was out forty-five minutes. Just about time enough to eat a little lunch of their own. I wonder they had any stomach for it.

5

I think you know I didn't find all that out during one hot October afternoon in the socn-to-be-defunct prison library, from one set of old newspapers stacked in a pair of Pomona orange cra-es, but I learned enough to make it hard for me to s-eep that night. When my wife got up at two in the morning and found me sitting in the kitchen, drinking buttermilk and smoking home-rolled Bugler, she asked me what was wrong and I lied to her for one of the few times in the long course of our marriage. I said I'd had another run-in with Percy Wetmore. I had, of course, but that wasn't the reason she'd found me sitting up late. I was usually able to leave Percy at the office.

"Well, forget that rotten apple and come on back to bed," she said. "I've got something that'll help you sleep, and you can have all you want."

"That sounds good, but I think we'd better not," I said. "I've got a little something wrong with my waterworks, and wouldn't want to pass it on to you."

She raised an eyebrow. "Waterworks, huh," she said. "I guess you must have taken up with the wrong streetcorner girl the last time you were in Baton Rouge." I've never been in Baton Rouge and never so much as touched a streetcorner girl, and we both knew it.

"It's just a plain old urinary infection," I said. "My mother used to say boys got them from taking a leak when the north wind was blowing."

"Your mother also used to stay in all day if she spilled the salt," my wife said. "Dr. Sadler—"

"No, sir," I said, raising my hand. "He'll want me to take sulfa, and I'll be throwing up in every corner of my office by the end of the week. It'll run its course, but in the meantime, I guess we best stay out of the playground."

She kissed my forehead right over my left eyebrow, which always gives me the prickles . . . as Janice well knew. "Poor baby. As if that awful Percy Wetmore wasn't enough. Come to bed soon."

I did, but before I did, I stepped out onto the back porch to empty out (and checked the wind direction with a wet thumb before I did—what our parents tell us when we are small seldom goes ignored, no matter how foolish it may be). Peeing outdoors is one joy of country living the poets never quite got around to, but it was no joy that night; the water coming out of me burned like a line of lit coal-oil. Yet I thought it had been a little worse that afternoon, and *knew* it had been worse the two or three days before. I had hopes that maybe I had started to mend. Never was a hope more ill-founded. No one had told me that sometimes a bug that gets up inside there, where it's warm and wet, can take a day or two off to rest before coming on strong again. I would have been surprised to know it. I would have been even more surprised to know that, in another fifteen or twenty years, there would be pills you could take that would smack that sort of infection out of your system in record time . . . and while those pills might make you feel a little sick at your stomach or loose in your bowels, they almost never made you vomit the way Dr. Sadler's sulfa pills did. Back in '32, there wasn't much you could do but wait, and try to ignore that feeling that someone had spilled coal-oil inside your works and then touched a match to it.

I finished my butt, went into the bedroom, and finally got to sleep. I dreamed of girls with shy smiles and blood in their hair.

6

The next morning there was a pink memo slip on my desk, asking me to stop by the warden's office as soon as I could. I knew what that was about—there were unwritten but very important rules to the game, and I had stopped playing by them for awhile yesterday—and so I put it off as long as possible. Like going to the doctor about my waterworks problem, I suppose. I've always thought this "get-it-over-with" business was overrated.

Anyway, I didn't hurry to Warden Moores's office. I stripped off my wool uniform coat instead, hung it over the back of my chair, and turned on the fan in the corner—it was another hot one. Then I sat down and went over Brutus Howell's night-sheet. There was nothing there to get alarmed about. Delacroix had wept briefly after turning in—he did most nights, and more for himself than for the folks he had roasted alive, I am quite sure—and then had taken Mr. Jingles, the mouse, out of the cigar box he slept in. That had calmed Del, and he had slept like a baby the rest of the night. Mr. Jingles had most likely spent it on Delacroix's stomach, with his tail curled over his paws, eyes unblinking. It was as if God had decided Delacroix needed a guardian angel, but had decreed in His wisdom that only a mouse would do for a rat like our homicidal friend from Louisiana. Not all *that* was in Brutal's report, of course, but I had done enough night watches myself to fill in the stuff between the lines. There was a brief note about Coffey: "Laid awake, mostly quiet, may have cried some. I tried to get some talk started, but after a few grunted replies from Coffey, gave up. Paul or Harry may have better luck."

"Getting the talk started" was at the center of our job, really. I didn't know it then, but looking back from the vantage point of this strange old age (I think all old ages seem strange to the folk who must endure them), I understand that it was, and why I didn't see it then—it was too big, as central to our work as our respiration was to our lives. It wasn't important that the floaters be good at "getting the talk started," but it was vital for me and Harry and Brutal and Dean . . . and it was one reason why Percy Wetmore was such a disaster. The inmates hated him, the guards hated him . . . everyone hated him, presumably, except for his political connections, Percy himself, and maybe (but only maybe) his mother. He was like a dose of white arsenic sprinkled into a wedding cake, and I think I knew he spelled disaster from the start. He was an accident waiting to happen. As for the rest of us, we would have scoffed at the idea that we functioned most usefully not as the guards of the condemned but as their psychiatrists—part of me still wants to scoff at that idea today—but we knew about getting the talk started . . . and without the talk, men facing Old Sparky had a nasty habit of going insane.

I made a note at the bottom of Brutal's report to talk to John Coffey—to try, at least—and then passed on to a note from Curtis Anderson, the warden's chief assistant. It said that he, Anderson, expected a DOE order for Edward Delacrois (Anderson's misspelling; the man's name was actually Eduard Delacroix) very soon. DOE stood for date of execution, and according to the note, Curtis had been told on good authority that the little Frenchman would take the walk shortly before Halloween—October 27th was his best guess, and Curtis Anderson's guesses were very informed. But before then we could expect a new resident, name of William Wharton. "He's what you like to call 'a problem child,'" Curtis had written in his back-slanting and somehow prissy script. "Crazy-wild and proud of it. Has rambled all over the state for the last year or so, and has hit the big time at last. Killed three people in a holdup, one a pregnant woman, killed a fourth in the getaway. State Patrolman. All he missed was a nun and a blind man." I smiled a little at that. "Wharton is 19 years old, has *Billy the Kid* tattooed on upper l. forearm. You will have to slap his nose a time or two, I guarantee you that, but be careful when you do it. <u>This man just doesn't care.</u>" He had underlined this last sentiment twice, then finished: "Also, he may be a hang-arounder. He's working appeals, and there's the fact that he is a minor."

A crazy kid, working appeals, apt to be around for awhile. Oh, that all sounded just fine. Suddenly the day seemed hotter than ever, and I could no longer put off seeing Warden Moores.

I worked for three wardens during my years as a Cold Mountain guard; Hal Moores was the last and best of them. In a walk. Honest, straightforward, lacking even Curtis Anderson's rudimentary wit, but equipped with just enough political savvy to keep his job during those grim years . . . and enough integrity to keep from getting seduced by the game. He would not rise any higher, but that seemed all right with him. He was fifty-eight or -nine back there, with a deeply lined bloodhound face that Bobo Marchant probably would have felt right at home with. He had white hair and his hands shook with some sort of palsy, but he was strong. The year before when a prisoner had rushed him in the exercise yard with a shank whittled out of a crate-slat, Moores had stood his ground, grabbed the skatehound's wrist and had twisted it so hard that the snapping bones had sounded like dry twigs burning in a hot fire. The skatehound, all his grievances forgotten, had gone down on his knees in the dirt and begun screaming for his mother. "I'm not her," Moores said in his cultured Southern voice, "but if I was, I'd raise up my skirts and piss on you from the loins that gave you birth."

When I came into his office, he started to get up and I waved him back down. I took the seat across the desk from him, and began by asking about his wife . . . except in our part of the world, that's not how you do it. "How's that pretty gal of yours?" is what I asked, as if Melinda had seen only seventeen summers instead of sixty-two or -three. My concern was genuine—she was a woman I could have loved and married myself, if the lines of our lives had coincided—but I didn't mind diverting him a little from his main business, either.

He sighed deeply. "Not so well, Paul. Not so well at all."

"More headaches?"

"Only one this week, but it was the worst yet—put her flat on her back for most of the day before yesterday. And now she's developed this weakness in her right hand—" He raised his own liverspotted right hand. We both watched it tremble above his blotter for a moment or two, and then he lowered it again. I could tell he would have given just about anything not to be telling me what he was telling me, and I would have given just about anything not to be hearing it. Melinda's headaches had started in the spring, and all that summer her doctor had been saying they were "nervous-tension migraines," perhaps caused by the stress of Hal's coming retirement. Except that neither of them could *wait* for his retirement, and my own wife had told me that migraine is not a disease of the old but the young; by the time its sufferers reached Melinda Moores's age, they were usually getting better, not worse. And now this weakness of the hand. It didn't sound like nervous tension to me; it sounded like a damned stroke.

"Dr. Haverstrom wants her to go in hospital up to Indianola," Moores said. "Have some tests. Head X-rays, he means. Who knows what else. She is scared to death." He paused, then added, "Truth to tell, so am I."

"Yeah, but you see she does it," I said. "Don't wait. If it turns out to be something they can see with an X-ray, it may turn out to be something they can fix."

"Yes," he agreed, and then, for just a moment—the only one during that part of our interview, as I recall—our eyes met and locked. There was the sort of nakedly perfect understanding between us that needs no words. It could be a stroke, yes. It could also be a cancer growing in her brain, and if it was that, the chances that the doctors at Indianola could do anything about it were slim going on none. This was '32, remember, when even something as relatively simple as a urinary infection was either sulfa and stink or suffer and wait.

"I thank you for your concern, Paul. Now let's talk about Percy Wetmore."

I groaned and covered my eyes.

"I had a call from the state capital this morning,"

the warden said evenly. "It was quite an angry call, as I'm sure you can imagine. Paul, the governor is so married he's almost not there, if you take my meaning. And his wife has a brother who has one child. That child is Percy Wetmore. Percy called his dad last night, and Percy's dad called Percy's aunt. Do I have to trace the rest of this out for you?"

"No," I said. "Percy squealed. Just like the schoolroom sissy telling teacher he saw Jack and Jill smooching in the cloakroom."

"Yep," Moores agreed, "that's about the size of it."

"You know what happened between Percy and Delacroix when Delacroix came in?" I asked. "Percy and his damned hickory billy-club?"

"Yes, but—"

"And you know how he runs it along the bars sometimes, just for the pure hell of it. He's mean, and he's stupid, and I don't know how much longer I can take him. That's the truth."

We'd known each other five years. That can be a long time for men who get on well, especially when part of the job is trading life for death. What I'm saying is that he understood what I meant. Not that I would quit; not with the Depression walking around outside the prison walls like a dangerous criminal, one that couldn't be caged as our charges were. Better men than me were out on the roads or riding the rods. I was lucky and knew it—children grown and the mortgage, that two-hundred-pound block of marble, had been off my chest for the last two years. But a man's got to eat, and his wife has to eat, too. Also, we were used to sending our daughter and son-in-law twenty bucks whenever we could afford it (and sometimes when we couldn't, if Jane's letters sounded particularly desperate). He was an out-of-work high-school teacher, and if that didn't qualify for desperate back in those days, then the word had no meaning. So no, you didn't walk off a steady-paycheck job like mine ... not in cold blood, that was. But my blood *wasn't* cold that fall. The temperatures outside were unseasonable, and the infection crawling around inside me had turned the thermostat up even more. And when a man's in that kind of situation, why, sometimes his fist flies out pretty much of its own accord. And if you slug a connected man like Percy Wetmore once, you might as well just go right on slugging, because there's no going back.

"Stick with it," Moores said quietly. "That's what I called you in here to say. I have it on good authority—the person who called me this morning, in fact—that Percy has an application in at Briar, and that his application will be accepted."

"Briar," I said. That was Briar Ridge, one of two state-run hospitals. "What's this kid doing? Touring state facilities?"

"It's an administration job. Better pay, and papers to push instead of hospital beds in the heat of the day." He gave me a slanted grin. "You know, Paul, you might be shed of him already if you hadn't put him in the switch-room with Van Hay when The Chief walked."

For a moment what he said seemed so peculiar I didn't have a clue what he was getting at. Maybe I didn't *want* to have a clue.

"Where else would I put him?" I asked. "Christ, he hardly knows what he's doing on the block! To make him part of the active execution team—" I didn't finish. Couldn't finish. The potential for screw-ups seemed endless.

"Nevertheless, you'd do well to put him out for Delacroix. If you want to get rid of him, that is."

I looked at him with my jaw hung. At last I was able to get it up where it belonged so I could talk. "What are you saying? That he wants to experience one right up close where he can smell the guy's nuts cooking?"

Moores shrugged. His eyes, so soft when he had been speaking about his wife, now looked flinty. "Delacroix's nuts are going to cook whether Wetmore's on the team or not," he said. "Correct?"

"Yes, but he could screw up. In fact, Hal, he's almost *bound* to screw up. And in front of thirty or so witnesses . . . reporters all the way up from Louisiana . . ."

"You and Brutus Howell will make sure he doesn't," Moores said. "And if he does anyway, it goes on his record, and it'll still be there long after his statehouse connections are gone. You understand?"

I did. It made me feel sick and scared, but I did.

"He may want to stay for Coffey, but if we're lucky, he'll get all he needs from Delacroix. You just make sure you put him out for that one."

I had planned to stick Percy in the switch-room again, then down in the tunnel, riding shotgun on the gurney that would take Delacroix to the meatwagon parked across the road from the prison, but I tossed all those plans back over my shoulder without so much as a second look. I nodded. I had the sense to know it was a gamble I was taking, but I didn't care. If it would get rid of Percy Wetmore, I'd tweak the devil's nose. He could take part in his execution, clamp on the cap, and then look through the grille and tell Van Hay to roll on two; he could watch the little Frenchman ride the lightning that he, Percy Wetmore, had let out of the bottle. Let him have his nasty little thrill, if that's what state-sanctioned murder was to him. Let him go on to Briar Ridge, where he would have his own office and a fan to cool it. And if his uncle by marriage was voted out of office in the next election and he had to find out what work was like in the tough old sunbaked world where not all the bad guys were locked behind bars and sometimes you got your own head whipped, so much the better.

"All right," I said, standing up. "I'll put him out front for Delacroix. And in the meantime, I'll keep the peace."

"Good," he said, and stood up himself. "By the

way, how's that problem of yours?" He pointed delicately in the direction of my groin.

"Seems a little better."

"Well, that's fine." He saw me to the door. "What about Coffey, by the way? Is he going to be a problem?"

"I don't think so," I said. "So far he's been as quiet as a dead rooster. He's strange—strange *eyes*—but quiet. We'll keep tabs on him, though. Don't worry about that."

"You know what he did, of course."

"Sure."

He was seeing me through to the outer office by then, where old Miss Hannah sat bashing away at her Underwood as she had ever since the last ice age had ended, it seemed. I was happy to go. All in all, I felt as if I'd gotten off easy. And it was nice to know there was a chance of surviving Percy, after all.

"You send Melinda a whole basket of my love," I said. "And don't go buying you an extra crate of trouble, either. It'll probably turn out to be nothing but migraine, after all."

"You bet," he said, and below his sick eyes, his lips smiled. The combination was damned near ghoulish.

As for me, I went back to E Block to start another day. There was paperwork to be read and written, there were floors to be mopped, there were meals to be served, a duty roster to be made out for the following week, there were a hundred details to be seen to. But mostly there was waiting—in prison there's always plenty of that, so much it never gets done. Waiting for Eduard Delacroix to walk the Green Mile, waiting for William Wharton to arrive with his curled lip and Billy the Kid tattoo, and, most of all, waiting for Percy Wetmore to be gone out of my life.

7

Delacroix's mouse was one of God's mysteries. I never saw one in E Block before that summer, and never saw one after that fall, when Delacroix passed from our company on a hot and thundery night in October—passed from it in a manner so unspeakable I can barely bring myself to recall it. Delacroix claimed that he trained that mouse, which started its life among us as Steamboat Willy, but I really think it was the other way around. Dean Stanton felt the same way, and so did Brutal. Both of them were there the night the mouse put in its first appearance, and as Brutal said, "The thing 'us half-tame already, and twice as smart as that Cajun what thought he owned it."

Dean and I were in my office, going over the record-box for the last year, getting ready to write follow-up letters to witnesses of five executions, and to write follow-ups to follow-ups in another six stretching all the way back to '29. Basically, we wanted to know just one thing: were they pleased with the service? I know it sounds grotesque, but it was an important consideration. As taxpayers they were our customers, but very special ones. A man or a woman who will turn out at midnight to watch a man die has got a special, pressing reason to be there, a special need, and if execution is a proper punishment, then that need ought to be satisfied. They've had a nightmare. The purpose of the execution is to show them that the nightmare is over. Maybe it even works that way. Sometimes.

"Hey!" Brutal called from outside the door, where he was manning the desk at the head of the hall. "Hey, you two! Get out here!"

Dean and I gazed at each other with identical expressions of alarm, thinking that something had happened to either the Indian from Oklahoma (his name was Arlen Bitterbuck, but we called him The Chief . . . or, in Harry Terwilliger's case, Chief Goat Cheese, because that was what Harry claimed Bitterbuck smelled like), or the fellow we called The President. But then Brutal started to laugh, and we hurried to see what was happening. Laughing in E Block sounded almost as wrong as laughing in church.

Old Toot-Toot, the trusty who ran the food-wagon in those days, had been by with his holy-rolling cartful of goodies, and Brutal had stocked up for a long night—three sandwiches, two pops, and a couple of moon pies. Also a side of potato salad Toot had undoubtedly filched from the prison kitchen, which was supposed to be off-limits to him. Brutal had the logbook open in front of him, and for a wonder he hadn't spilled anything on it yet. Of course, he was just getting started.

"What?" Dean asked. "What is it?"

"State legislature must have opened the purse-strings enough to hire another screw this year after all," Brutal said, still laughing. "Lookie yonder."

He pointed and we saw the mouse. I started to laugh, too, and Dean joined in. You really couldn't help it, because a guard doing quarter-hour check rounds was just like that mouse looked like: a tiny, furry guard making sure no one was trying to escape or commit suicide. It would trot a little way toward us along the Green Mile, then turn its head from side to side, as if checking the cells. Then it would make another forward spurt. The fact that we could hear both of our current inmates snoring away in spite of the yelling and the laughter somehow made it even funnier.

It was a perfectly ordinary brown mouse, except for the way it seemed to be checking into the cells. It even went into one or two of them, skipping nimbly in between the lower bars in a way I imagine many of our inmates, past and present, would envy. Except it was *out* that the cons would always be wanting to skip, of course.

The mouse didn't go into either of the occupied cells; only the empties. And finally it had worked its way almost up to where we were. I kept expecting it to turn back, but it didn't. It showed no fear of us at all.

"It ain't normal for a mouse to come up on people that way," Dean said, a little nervously. "Maybe it's rabid."

"Oh, my Christ," Brutal said through a mouthful of corned-beef sandwich. "The big mouse expert. The Mouse Man. You see it foamin at the mouth, Mouse Man?"

"I can't see its mouth at all," Dean said, and that made us all laugh again. I couldn't see its mouth, either, but I could see the dark little drops that were its eyes, and they didn't look crazy or rabid to me. They looked interested and intelligent. I've put men to death—men with supposedly immortal souls—that looked dumber than that mouse.

It scurried up the Green Mile to a spot that was less than three feet from the duty desk ... which wasn't something fancy, like you might be imagining, but only the sort of desk the teachers used to sit behind up at the district high school. And there it did stop, curling its tail around its paws as prim as an old lady settling her skirts.

I stopped laughing all at once, suddenly feeling cold through my flesh all the way to the bones. I want to say I don't know why I felt that way—no one likes to come out with something that's going to make them look or sound ridiculous—but of course I do, and if I can tell the truth about the rest, I guess I can tell the truth about this. For a moment I imagined myself to be that mouse, not a guard at all but just another convicted criminal there on the Green Mile, convicted and condemned but still managing to look bravely up at a desk that must have seemed miles high to it (as the judgment seat of God will no doubt someday seem to us), and at the heavy-voiced, blue-coated giants who sat behind it. Giants that shot its kind with BB guns, or swatted them with brooms, or set traps on them, traps that broke their backs while they crept cautiously over the word VICTOR to nibble at the cheese on the little copper plate.

There was no broom by the duty desk, but there was a rolling mop-bucket with the mop still in the wringer; I'd taken my turn at swabbing the green lino and all six of the cells shortly before sitting down to the record-box with Dean. I saw that Dean meant to grab the mop and take a swing with it. I touched his wrist just as his fingers touched the slender wooden handle. "Leave it be," I said.

He shrugged and drew his hand back. I had a feeling he didn't want to swat it any more than I did.

Brutal tore a corner off his corned-beef sandwich and held it out over the front of the desk, tweezed delicately between two fingers. The mouse seemed to look up with an even livelier interest, as if it knew exactly what it was. Probably did; I could see its whiskers twitch as its nose wriggled.

"Aw, Brutal, no!" Dean exclaimed, then looked at me. "Don't let him do that, Paul! If he's gonna feed the damn thing, we might as well put out the welcome mat for anything on four legs."

"I just want to see what he'll do," Brutal said. "In the interests of science, like." He looked at me—I was the boss, even in such minor detours from routine as this. I thought about it and shrugged like it didn't matter much, one way or another. The truth was, I kind of wanted to see what he'd do, too.

Well, he ate it—of course. There was a Depression on, after all. But the *way* he ate it fascinated us all. He approached the fragment of sandwich, sniffed his way around it, and then he sat up in front of it like a dog doing a trick, grabbed it, and pulled the bread apart to get at the meat. He did it as deliberately and knowingly as a man tucking into a good roast-beef dinner in his favorite restaurant. I never saw an animal eat like that, not even a well-trained house dog. And all the while he was eating, his eyes never left us.

"Either one smart mouse or hungry as hell," a new voice said. It was Bitterbuck. He had awakened and now stood at the bars of his cell, naked except for a pair of saggy-seated boxer shorts. A home-rolled cigarette poked out from between the second and third knuckles of his right hand, and his iron-gray hair lay over his shoulders—once probably muscular but now beginning to soften—in a pair of braids.

"You got any Injun wisdom about micies, Chief?" Brutal asked, watching the mouse eat. We were all pretty fetched by the neat way it held the bit of corned beef in its forepaws, occasionally turning it or glancing at it, as if in admiration and appreciation.

"Naw," Bitterbuck said. "Knowed a brave once had a pair of what he claimed were mouse-skin gloves, but I didn't believe it." Then he laughed, as if the whole thing was a joke, and left the bars. We heard the bunk creak as he lay down again.

That seemed to be the mouse's signal to go. It finished up what it was holding, sniffed at what was left (mostly bread with yellow mustard soaking into it), and then looked back at us, as if it wanted to remember our faces if we met again. Then it turned and scurried off the way it had come, not pausing to do any cell-checks this time. Its hurry made me think of the White Rabbit in *Alice's Adventures in Wonderland*, and I smiled. It didn't pause at the door to the restraint room, but disappeared beneath it. The restraint room had soft walls, for people whose brains had softened a little. We kept cleaning equipment stored in there when we didn't need the room for its created purpose, and a few books (most were westerns by Clarence Mulford, but one—loaned out only on special occasions—featured a profusely illustrated tale in which Popeye, Bluto, and even Wimpy the hamburger fiend took turns shtupping Olive Oyl). There were craft items as well, including the crayons Delacroix later put to some good use. Not that he was our problem yet; this was earlier, remember. Also in the restraint room was the jacket no one wanted to wear—white, made of double-sewn canvas, and with the buttons and snaps and buckles going up the back. We all knew how to zip a problem child into that jacket lickety-larrup. They didn't get violent often, our lost boys, but when they did, brother, you didn't wait around for the situation to improve on its own.

Brutal reached into the desk drawer above the kneehole and brought out the big leather-bound book with the word VISITORS stamped on the front in gold leaf. Ordinarily, that book stayed in the drawer from one month to the next. When a prisoner had visitors—unless it was a lawyer or a minister—he went over to the room off the messhall that was kept special for that purpose. The Arcade, we called it. I don't know why.

"Just what in the Gorry do you think *you're* doing?" Dean Stanton asked, peering over the tops of his spectacles as Brutal opened the book and paged grandly past years of visitors to men now dead.

"Obeyin Regulation 19," Brutal said, finding the current page. He took the pencil and licked the tip—a disagreeable habit of which he could not be broken—and prepared to write. Regulation 19 stated simply: "Each visitor to E Block shall show a yellow Administration pass and shall be recorded *without fail.*"

"He's gone nuts," Dean said to me.

"He didn't show us his pass, but I'm gonna let it go this time," Brutal said. He gave the tip of his pencil an extra lick for good luck, then filled in 9:49 p.m. under the column headed TIME ON BLOCK.

"Sure, why not, the big bosses probably make exceptions for mice," I said.

"Course they do," Brutal agreed. "Lack of pockets." He turned to look at the wall-clock behind the desk, then printed 10:01 in the column headed TIME OFF BLOCK. The longer space between these two numbers was headed NAME OF VISITOR. After a moment's hard thought—probably to muster his limited spelling skills, as I'm sure the idea was in his head already—Brutus Howell carefully wrote STEAMBOAT WILLY, which was what most people called Mickey Mouse back in those days. It was because of that first talkie cartoon, where he rolled his eyes and bumped his hips around and pulled the whistle cord in the pilothouse of the steamboat.

"There," Brutal said, slamming the book closed and returning it to its drawer, "all done and buttoned up."

I laughed, but Dean, who couldn't help being serious about things even when he saw the joke, was frowning and polishing his glasses furiously. "You'll be in trouble if someone sees that." He hesitated and added, "The wrong someone." He hesitated again, looking nearsightedly around almost as if he expected to see that the walls had grown ears, before finishing: "Someone like Percy Kiss-My-Ass-and-Go-to-Heaven Wetmore."

"Huh," Brutal said. "The day Percy Wetmore sits

his narrow shanks down here at this desk will be the day I resign."

"You won't have to," Dean said. "They'll fire you for making jokes in the visitors' book if Percy puts the right word in the right ear. And he can. You know he can."

Brutal glowered but said nothing. I reckoned that later on that night he would erase what he had written. And if he didn't, I would.

The next night, after getting first Bitterbuck and then The President over to D Block, where we showered our group after the regular cons were locked down, Brutal asked me if we shouldn't have a look for Steamboat Willy down there in the restraint room.

"I guess we ought to," I said. We'd had a good laugh over that mouse the night before, but I knew that if Brutal and I found it down there in the restraint room—particularly if we found it had gnawed itself the beginnings of a nest in one of the padded walls—we would kill it. Better to kill the scout, no matter how amusing it might be, than have to live with the pilgrims. And, I shouldn't have to tell you, neither of us was very squeamish about a little mouse-murder. Killing rats was what the state paid us for, after all.

But we didn't find Steamboat Willy—later to be known as Mr. Jingles—that night, not nested in the soft walls, or behind any of the collected junk we hauled out into the corridor. There was a great deal of junk, too, more than I would have expected, because we hadn't had to use the restraint room in a long time. That would change with the advent of William Wharton, but of course we didn't know that at the time. Lucky us.

"Where'd it go?" Brutal asked at last, wiping sweat off the back of his neck with a big blue bandanna. "No hole, no crack . . . there's that, but—" He pointed to the drain in the floor. Below the grate, which the mouse could have gotten through, was a fine steel mesh that not even a fly would have passed. "How'd it get in? How'd it get out?"

"I don't know," I said.

"He *did* come in here, didn't he? I mean, the three of us saw him."

"Yep, right under the door. He had to squeeze a little, but he made it."

"Gosh," Brutal said—a word that sounded strange, coming from a man that big. "It's a good thing the cons can't make themselves small like that, isn't it?"

"You bet," I said, running my eye over the canvas walls one last time, looking for a hole, a crack, anything. There was nothing. "Come on. Let's go."

Steamboat Willy showed up again three nights later, when Harry Terwilliger was on the duty desk. Percy was also on, and chased the mouse back down the Green Mile with the same mop Dean had been thinking of using. The rodent avoided Percy easily, slipping through the crack beneath the restraint-room door a hands-down winner. Cursing at the top of his voice, Percy unlocked the door and hauled all that shit out again. It was funny and scary at the same time, Harry said. Percy was vowing he'd catch the goddam mouse and tear its diseased little head right off, but he didn't, of course. Sweaty and disheveled, the shirttail of his uniform hanging out in the back, he returned to the duty desk half an hour later, brushing his hair out of his eyes and telling Harry (who had sat serenely reading through most of the ruckus) that he was going to put a strip of insulation on the bottom of the door down there; *that* would solve the vermin problem, he declared.

"Whatever you think is best, Percy," Harry said, turning a page of the oat opera he was reading. He thought Percy would forget about blocking the crack at the bottom of that door, and he was right.

8

Late that winter, long after these events were over, Brutal came to me one night when it was just the two of us, E Block temporarily empty and all the other guards temporarily reassigned. Percy had gone on to Briar Ridge.

"Come here," Brutal said in a funny, squeezed voice that made me look around at him sharply. I had just come in out of a cold and sleety night, and had been brushing off the shoulders of my coat prior to hanging it up.

"Is something wrong?" I asked.

"No," he said, "but I found out where Mr. Jingles was staying. When he first came, I mean, before Delacroix took him over. Do you want to see?"

Of course I did. I followed him down the Green Mile to the restraint room. All the stuff we kept stored there was out in the hall; Brutal had apparently taken advantage of the lull in customer traffic to do some cleaning up. The door was open, and I saw our mop-bucket inside. The floor, that same sick lime shade as the Green Mile itself, was drying in streaks. Standing in the middle of the floor was a stepladder, the one that was usually kept in the storage room, which also happened to serve as the final stop for the state's condemned. There was a shelf jutting out from the back of the ladder near the top, the sort of thing a workman would use to hold his toolkit or a painter the bucket he was working out of. There was a flashlight on it. Brutal handed it to me.

"Get on up there. You're shorter than me, so you'll have to go pretty near all the way, but I'll hold your legs."

"I'm ticklish down there," I said, starting up. "Especially my knees."

"I'll mind that."

"Good," I said, "because a broken hip's too high a price to pay in order to discover the origins of a single mouse."

"Huh?"

"Never mind." My head was up by the caged light in the center of the ceiling by then, and I could feel the ladder wiggling a little under my weight. Outside, I could hear the winter wind moaning. "Just hold onto me."

"I got you, don't worry." He gripped my calves firmly, and I went up one more step. Now the top of my head was less than a foot from the ceiling, and I could see the cobwebs a few enterprising spiders had spun in the crotches where the roof beams came together. I shone the light around but didn't see anything worth the risk of being up here.

"No," Brutal said. "You're looking too far away, Paul. Look to your left, where those two beams come together. You see them? One's a little discolored."

"I see."

"Shine the light on the join."

I did, and saw what he wanted me to see almost right away. The beams had been pegged together with dowels, half a dozen of them, and one was gone, leaving a black, circular hole the size of a quarter. I looked at it, then looked doubtfully back over my shoulder at Brutal. "It was a small mouse," I said, "but that small? Man, I don't think so."

"But that's where he went," Brutal said. "I'm just as sure as houses."

"I don't see how you can be."

"Lean closer—don't worry, I got you—and take a whiff."

I did as he asked, groping with my left hand for one of the other beams, and feeling a little better when I had hold of it. The wind outside gusted again; air puffed out of that hole and into my face. I could smell the keen breath of a winter night in the border South . . . and something else, as well.

The smell of peppermint.

Don't let nothing happen to Mr. Jingles, I could hear Delacroix saying in a voice that wouldn't stay steady. I could hear that, and I could feel the warmth of Mr. Jingles as the Frenchman handed it to me, just a mouse, smarter than most of the species, no doubt, but still just a mouse for a' that and a' that. *Don't let that bad 'un hurt my mouse*, he'd said, and I had promised, as I always promised them at the end, when walking the Green Mile was no longer a myth or a hypothesis but something they really had to do. Mail this letter to my brother, who I haven't seen for twenty years? I promise. Say fifteen Hail Marys for my soul? I promise. Let me die under my spirit-name and see that it goes on my tombstone? I promise. It was the way you got them to go and be good about it, the way you saw them into the chair sitting at the end of the Green Mile with their sanity intact. I couldn't keep all of those promises, of course, but I kept the one I made to Delacroix. As for the Frenchman himself, there had been hell to pay. The bad 'un had hurt Delacroix, hurt him plenty. Oh, I know what he did, all right, but no one deserved what happened to Eduard Delacroix when he fell into Old Sparky's savage embrace.

A smell of peppermint.

And something else. Something back inside that hole.

I took a pen out of my breast pocket with my right hand, still holding onto the beam with my left, not worried anymore about Brutal inadvertently tickling my sensitive knees. I unscrewed the pen's cap one-handed, then poked the nib in and teased something out. It was a tiny splinter of wood which had been tinted a bright yellow, and I heard Delacroix's voice again, so clearly this time that his ghost might have been lurking in that room with us—the one where William Wharton spent so much of his time.

Hey, you guys! the voice said this time—the laughing, amazed voice of a man who has forgotten, at least for a little while, where he is and what awaits him. *Come and see what Mr. Jingles can do!*

"Christ," I whispered. I felt as if the wind had been knocked out of me.

"You found another one, didn't you?" Brutal asked. "I found three or four."

I came down and shone the light on his big, outstretched palm. Several splinters of wood were scattered there, like jackstraws for elves. Two were yellow, like the one I had found. One was green and one was red. They hadn't been painted but colored, with wax Crayola crayons.

"Oh, boy," I said in a low, shaky voice. "Oh, hey. It's pieces of that spool, isn't it? But why? Why up there?"

"When I was a kid I wasn't big like I am now," Brutal said. "I got most of my growth between fifteen and seventeen. Until then I was a shrimp. And when I went off to school the first time, I felt as small as . . . why, as small as a mouse, I guess you'd say. I was scared to death. So you know what I did?"

I shook my head. Outside, the wind gusted again. In the angles formed by the beams, cobwebs shook in feathery drafts, like rotted lace. Never had I been in a place that felt so nakedly haunted, and it was right then, as we stood there looking down at the splintered remains of the spool which had caused so much trouble, that my head began to know what my heart had understood ever since John Coffey had walked the Green Mile: I couldn't do this job much longer. Depression or no Depression, I couldn't watch many more men walk through my office to their deaths. Even one more might be too many.

"I asked my mother for one of her hankies," Brutal said. "So when I felt weepy and small, I could sneak it out and smell her perfume and not feel so bad."

"You think—what?—that mouse chewed off some of that colored spool to remember Delacroix by? That a *mouse*—"

He looked up. I thought for a moment I saw tears in his eyes, but I guess I was probably wrong about that. "I ain't saying nothing, Paul. But I found them up there, and I smelled peppermint, same as you—you know you did. And I can't do this no more. I *won't* do this no more. Seeing one more man in that chair'd just about kill me. I'm going to put in for a transfer to Boys' Correctional on Monday. If I get it before the next one, that's fine. If I don't, I'll resign and go back to farming."

"What did you ever farm, besides rocks?"

"It don't matter."

"I know it doesn't," I said. "I think I'll put in with you."

He looked at me close, making sure I wasn't just having some sport with him, then nodded as if it was a settled thing. The wind gusted again, strong enough this time to make the beams creak and settle, and we both looked around uneasily at the padded walls. I think for a moment we could hear William Wharton—not Billy the Kid, not him, he had been "Wild Bill" to us from his first day on the block— screaming and laughing, telling us we were going to be damned glad to be rid of him, telling us we would never forget him. About those things he was right.

As for what Brutal and I agreed on that night in the restraint room, it turned out just that way. It was almost as if we had taken a solemn oath on those tiny bits of colored wood. Neither of us ever took part in another execution. John Coffey was the last.

To Be Continued

THE GREAT ESCAPE

Stay tuned to *The Green Mile* serial thriller for your chance to WIN over 1,000 AIR MILES awards in each episode up to Part 5, with a massive 6,000 AIR MILES awards to be won in Part 6 for the greatest escape ever!

COMPETITION No.1

WIN **1001** AIR MILES AWARDS PLUS A
SPECIAL EDITION OF THE NEXT EPISODE
Mouse on the Mile SIGNED BY STEPHEN KING

Call 0881 88 77 66

with your answers to the following questions and you could escape to a destination of your choice.

Which of the following events will happen in the next episode...

1. Brutus "Brutal" Howell is found murdered.

2. Chief Arlen Bitterbuck goes to the electric chair.

3. William "Wild Bill" Wharton is found hanging in his cell.

Tie Breaker:

In 20 words or less, describe the continuing plot of *The Green Mile*...

Telephone lines close MIDNIGHT 18 April 1996

The serial thriller
continues next month . . .

STEPHEN KING'S
THE GREEN MILE:
Part Two
The Mouse on the Mile

Cold Mountain has always been home to many of life's troubled souls. Sometimes they live behind bars, awaiting the ultimate punishment. Others parade the dank halls, guarding the inmates with a terrible vengeance. And sometimes salvation comes from the most unlikely source . . .

To Be Continued . . .

Visit *The Green Mile* on the Internet!
http://www.greenmile.com/usa/